Let's Go
APPLE PICKING!

By Lori Haskins Houran
Illustrated by Nila Aye

🌹 A GOLDEN BOOK · NEW YORK

rhcbooks.com
Educators and librarians, for a variety of teaching tools, visit us at RHTeachersLibrarians.com
Library of Congress Control Number: 2019930827
ISBN 978-0-593-12325-6 (trade) — ISBN 978-0-593-12326-3 (ebook)
Printed in the United States of America
10 9 8 7 6 5 4 3 2 1

Every Saturday, I go to Grandpa's house. Every Saturday, we eat the same snack—apple slices and peanut butter.

"Uh-oh, Grandpa," I said last Saturday. "We're out of apples."

"Is that so?" said Grandpa. "We'd better get some more."

We got in the car. But Grandpa drove right past the grocery store! He took us way out of town, to a big red barn on a hill.

"Let's go apple picking!" he said.

I ran to the barn. Grandpa was right behind me.

"Good morning, folks." A boy gave us a basket to fill with apples.

TOOT, TOOT. A tractor pulled up. It was
tugging a wagon full of hay.
"Hop on," said the farmer. "I'll give you a ride
to the orchard."

The hayride was bumpy. Scratchy, too.
I loved it!

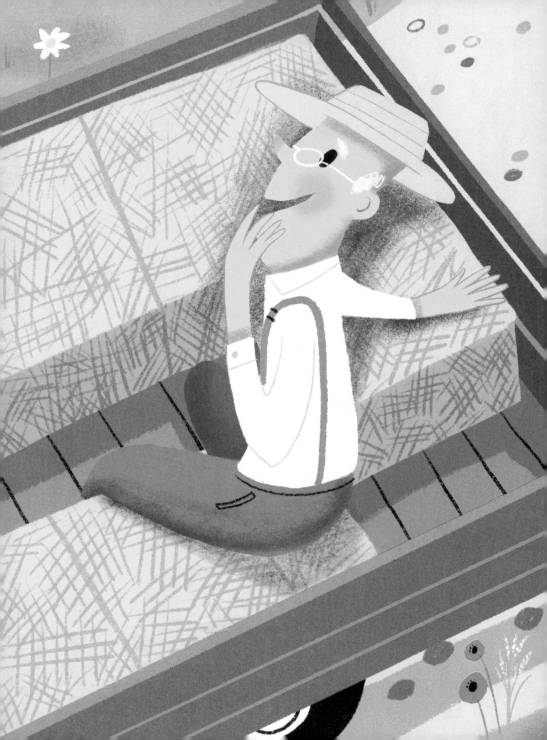

"Here you are," the farmer called.

I sat up. All I saw were trees. Rows and rows of them. Each tree was full of apples!

Red ones. Green ones. Pink ones. Gold ones.

"Which kind should we pick?" I asked
Grandpa.
"How about some of each?" he said.
Grandpa is so smart.

The farmer showed us what to do.
"Twist an apple up toward the sky," she said.
"Then tug. If the apple stays put, it's not ripe.
If it pops off, it's ready to eat."

I gave it a try.
Twist. Tug. *POP!*
A pretty red apple came right off the tree.

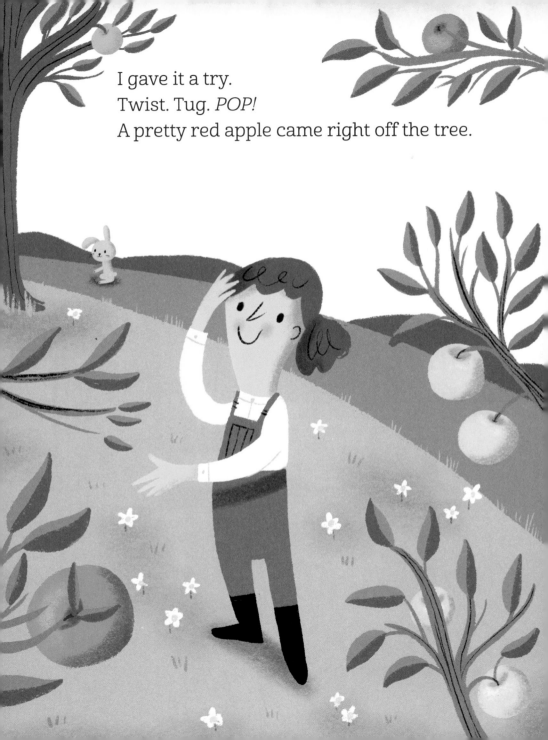

Grandpa and I made a good team. I picked the apples on the high branches. He got the ones down low.

It took a long time, but we filled our basket
to the top.

The farmer helped us lift our basket into the wagon.

"We'll take the long way back to the barn," she said. "I have some friends you might like to meet."

I met a goat, some sheep, and two ponies!
One pony ate an apple right out of my hand.
I could have stayed there forever.

Only . . . what was that delicious smell?

"Apple cider time!" said Grandpa. He ordered two cups, with extra cinnamon sticks.

The cider was warm and sweet. We drank it all up.

"I'm not thirsty anymore," Grandpa said. "But I *am* a little hungry."

"Me too," I said. "Let's go have our snack, Grandpa."

We paid for our apples and said goodbye.

At Grandpa's house, I washed two of our apples. Grandpa cut them up and put peanut butter on the slices.

We ate our snack, the same way we do every Saturday.

We licked our fingers, the same way we do every Saturday.

And Grandpa told me the same thing he says
every Saturday:

"You're the apple of my eye!"